STO

This book
belongs to:

Colin and Neila

Francis and the First Nativity

Written by
L. E. McCullough

Illustrated by
Maggie Swanson

Regina
Press

On the lawn outside our church
at Christmastime each year,
there stands a scene of beauty
that brings our town much cheer.

The stable and the figures
of the Nativity,
remind us of Saint Francis
and how they came to be.

About nine hundred years ago,
in a small Italian town,
there lived this kind and gentle man
of very great renown.

Francis of Assisi
wanted everyone to know
how God sent his Son to earth,
so many years ago.

Francis told a faithful friend---
Giovanni was his name---
"Go to the town of Greccio
atop the mountain plain."

"Gather all the animals,
fill the crib with straw and hay,
make ready for the baby
as in Bethlehem that day."

Each piece of wood, each nail and board
was shaped with craft and care,
to welcome Mary and Joseph
and the Babe who would lie there.

On a snowy Christmas Eve,
beneath the starry sky,
Francis led the villagers
to the mountainside up high.

"This is how the Christ Child came!"
Francis cried out to the throng.
"Greet Him with grateful prayers
and sing some joyful songs."

"He came to earth, a tiny child,
of parents poor and plain,
to show how much He loves you
and to share your joy and pain."

Krippe – Germany

Nacimeinto – Latin America

Szopka – Poland

Creche - France

Now people all around the world
make their Nativity scene,
to enable them to see and feel
the wonder that had been.

Presepio - Italy

The Nativity in church and home,
helps us to understand
what Jesus' birth really means
according to God's plan.

He came to earth from God,
our Father in Heaven above,
to show us how He loves us
and to teach us how to love.